The Family Of Deception

The Shadow series, Volume 1

Allan De Genius

Published by Allan Inspirations, 2024.

This is a work of fiction. Similarities to real people, places, or events are entirely coincidental.

THE FAMILY OF DECEPTION

First edition. November 1, 2024.

Copyright © 2024 Allan De Genius.

ISBN: 979-8227869616

Written by Allan De Genius.

Table of Contents

PROLOGUE 1
CHAPTER ONE 2
CHAPTER TWO 7
CHAPTER THREE 12
CHAPTER FOUR 15
CHAPTER FIVE 18
CHAPTER SIX 22
CHAPTER SEVEN 25
CHAPTER EIGHT 27
CHAPTER NINE 30
CHAPTER TEN 33
CHAPTER ELEVEN 36
CHAPTER TWELVE 39
CHAPTER THIRTEEN 42
CHAPTER FOURTEEN 45
CHAPTER FIFTEEN 47
CHAPTER SIXTEEN 49
CHAPTER SEVENTEEN 51
CHAPTER EIGHTEEN 54
CHAPTER NINETEEN 56
CHAPTER TWENTY 59
EPILOGUE 63

For those who have ever felt the weight of secret and lies.

"The Lies We Tell Ourselves Are The Most Damaging Of All"

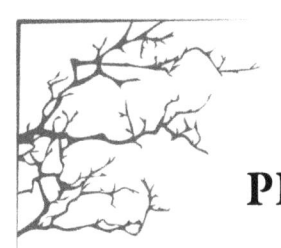

PROLOGUE

I stared at the headline, the words searing into my soul like a branding iron: "Billionaire Philanthropist Charged with Embezzlement. Family Empire Crumbles."

My father's face, once a symbol of integrity and strength, now stared back at me from the newspaper, his eyes haunted by the weight of his own deceit. The man who had taught me to ride a bike, to play chess, and to never tell a lie had been living a lie.

A chill crept up my spine as I read the devastating truth. My family's philanthropic foundation, renowned for its charitable work, was a facade. A cleverly crafted scheme to funnel millions into my father's secret accounts.

"Mom?" I whispered, searching for answers, but she stood frozen, her eyes fixed on the same headline, her expression a mixture of shock, shame, and desperation.

"It's not what you think, Ava," she stammered, but I knew better. I knew that nothing would ever be the same again.

In that moment, my world shattered, leaving me with more questions than answers. Who was my father, really? What else had he lied about? And how far would he go to keep his secrets safe?

CHAPTER ONE

3:04 AM

The phone rang, shrill and insistent, shattering the fragile peace of my sleep. I groggily reached for the receiver, my heart racing with a sense of foreboding. Who could be calling at this ungodly hour? My mind instantly went to my father, August Blackwood. Was something wrong? Had something happened to him?

I hesitated for a moment before answering, my voice barely above a whisper. "Hello?"

"Ava, it's Rachel." My father's personal assistant's voice was tight, laced with an undercurrent of urgency. "I'm so sorry to wake you, but...your father needs you."

My gut twisted into a knot. Needs me? What did that even mean? My father never needed anyone.

"What's going on, Rachel?" I demanded, throwing off the covers and swinging my legs over the side of the bed.

"I'm not entirely sure," Rachel hedged. "Your father just called me, said he had to see you immediately. He sounded...different, Ava. Scared, maybe."

A chill ran down my spine. My father, scared? That was unthinkable.

"Where is he?" I asked, already grabbing my clothes and heading for the closet.

"He's at the estate. He wants you to come now."

I nodded, even though Rachel couldn't see me. "I'm on my way."

As I hung up the phone, my mind began racing. What could be so urgent that my father needed me in the middle of the night? And what was Rachel hiding?

I quickly dressed and grabbed my keys, my heart pounding in anticipation. This was more than just a family emergency – it felt like a warning sign.

The city streets were deserted as I sped toward the Blackwood Estate, the GPS guiding me through the dark. My thoughts drifted back to my childhood, growing up within those opulent walls.

The estate loomed before me, its turrets and grand facade illuminated by the moon. I pulled up to the entrance, and the gates swung open, admitting me to the world I'd thought I'd left behind.

As I stepped into the foyer, a chill greeted me. The chandelier above cast eerie shadows on the walls.

"Ava." Rachel emerged from the shadows, her face pinched with worry.

"Where's my father?" I asked, scanning the empty hallway.

Rachel hesitated. "He's...waiting for you. In his study."

I took a deep breath and headed toward the study, my heart heavy with foreboding.

I pushed open the study door, and a warm glow enveloped me. My father sat behind his massive mahogany desk, his eyes fixed on the papers scattered before him. His usual calm demeanor was replaced by a look of agitation.

"Ava, thank you for coming," he said, his voice low and gravelly.

I approached the desk, my senses on high alert. "What's going on, Father? Rachel said you needed me."

He looked up, his eyes locking onto mine. For a moment, I saw something there, something that looked almost like...fear.

"I've received some disturbing news," he began, his voice measured. "News that affects our family's reputation, our business...everything."

My mind began racing. What could possibly threaten the Blackwood Empire?

"Tell me," I urged, my voice firm.

He hesitated, then handed me a folder filled with documents. "Read this."

As I scanned the pages, my heart sank. The words blurred together, but one phrase stood out: "embezzlement," "fraud," and "Blackwood Industries."

"No," I whispered, feeling like I'd been punched in the gut.

My father's expression turned grim. "It's true, Ava. Someone has been manipulating our finances, siphoning off millions."

I felt a wave of nausea wash over me. Who could do this? And why?

"We need to find out who's behind this," I said, determination rising within me.

My father nodded. "I agree. But there's more."

He paused, his eyes darting around the room as if searching for an escape.

"What is it?" I pressed.

"I think...I think it's someone close to us."

My world tilted. Someone close to us? That meant...

THE FAMILY OF DECEPTION

"A family member?" I whispered.

He nodded, his face etched with pain.

I stumbled backward, reeling from the implications. Who could betray us like this?

As I stood there, the weight of my father's words settled upon me like a physical force, crushing the very air from my lungs.

"Someone close to us," I repeated, the phrase echoing through my mind like a curse.

My father's eyes, once bright and commanding, now seemed dull and haunted, as if the shadows themselves were closing in around him.

"Ava, I need your help," he said, his voice barely above a whisper, yet carrying the weight of a thousand unspoken truths.

I felt a shiver run down my spine as I met his gaze, the connection between us crackling with an unspoken understanding.

"What do you want me to do?" I asked, my voice firm, yet laced with a hint of trepidation.

He leaned forward, his elbows resting on the desk, his hands clasped together in a gesture of supplication.

"I want you to find out who's behind this," he said, his eyes burning with a fierce determination.

I nodded, my mind already racing with possibilities, scenarios, and suspects.

But as I turned to leave, his words stopped me cold.

"Ava?"

I turned back, my heart pounding in anticipation.

"Be careful," he said, his voice low and urgent.

"Why?" I asked, my instincts screaming warning.

"Because," he paused, his eyes locking onto mine, "I think we're running out of time."

The words hung in the air, a challenge, a warning, and a promise. And I knew, in that moment, that nothing would ever be the same again.

CHAPTER TWO

As I left my father's study, the weight of his words settled upon me like a physical burden. Who could be behind the embezzlement? And what did my father mean by "we're running out of time"?

I couldn't shake off the feeling that I was missing something. Something big.

I made my way to the kitchen, seeking the comfort of familiar surroundings. Rachel was already there, brewing coffee.

"Ava, what did your father say?" she asked, her eyes filled with concern.

I hesitated, unsure how much to reveal. "He thinks someone close to us is behind the embezzlement."

Rachel's expression turned pale. "That's impossible. Who would do such a thing?"

I shrugged. "That's what I need to find out."

As we sipped our coffee, I noticed Rachel's nervous glances. Was she hiding something?

"Rachel, do you know anything about the embezzlement?" I asked, my tone firm.

She shook her head vigorously. "No, Ava. I swear. I had no idea."

But her eyes told a different story.

As I stood in the kitchen, surrounded by the warm, golden light of dawn, I couldn't shake off the feeling of unease that had settled within me. The weight of my father's words, like an unspoken accusation, hung in the air, casting a pall of suspicion over everyone I knew.

Rachel's eyes, once bright and open, now seemed shrouded in secrecy, her gaze darting around the room like a trapped animal searching for escape. I sensed a fragility in her demeanor, a vulnerability that belied her usual composed exterior.

"Rachel, I need to ask you something," I said, my voice low and measured, as I pulled out a chair and sat beside her.

She turned to me, her expression wary. "What is it, Ava?"

"Do you know anything about the embezzlement?" I asked, my eyes locking onto hers, searching for any sign of deception.

Rachel's face paled, her skin taking on a translucent quality. "No, Ava. I swear. I had no idea."

But her words, though fervent, lacked conviction. I detected a faint tremble in her voice, a hesitation that spoke volumes.

"Rachel, I need the truth," I pressed, my tone firm but gentle.

She looked away, her gaze drifting toward the window, where the morning light cast an eerie glow on the gardens below.

"I don't know what you're talking about," she whispered, her voice barely audible.

I reached out, my hand covering hers. "Rachel, I know you're hiding something. Please, tell me."

For a moment, our eyes locked, the tension between us palpable. Then, like a shutter closing, Rachel's expression changed, her mask slipping back into place.

"I'm telling you the truth, Ava," she said, her voice flat.

But I knew better. I knew that Rachel was concealing something, something that could shatter the very foundations of our family's empire.

As I gazed into Rachel's eyes, I sensed a depth of emotion that made my heart ache. Her secrets, like hidden currents, rippled beneath the surface, threatening to pull me under.

"What are you afraid of, Rachel?" I asked, my voice barely above a whisper.

Rachel's mask slipped, revealing a glimmer of desperation. "I'm afraid of losing everything," she whispered. "My job, my reputation...my family."

I felt a pang of empathy. Rachel's loyalty to our family was unwavering, but at what cost?

"Why are you protecting someone, Rachel?" I pressed, my words gentle but insistent.

Rachel's eyes darted around the room, as if searching for an escape. "I'm not protecting anyone," she insisted.

But I knew better. I saw the fear etched on her face, the weight of secrets bearing down on her.

"Rachel, I need to know the truth," I urged, my hand covering hers. "Who's behind the embezzlement?"

Rachel's gaze snapped back to mine, her eyes flashing with a mixture of fear and defiance.

"You don't understand, Ava," she said, her voice trembling. "This goes deeper than you think. It's not just about money...it's about power."

A shiver ran down my spine. Power? What did Rachel mean?

"Tell me," I coaxed, my voice soft.

Rachel's lips parted, as if to speak, but then she clamped them shut.

"I can't," she whispered. "I'm sorry, Ava."

I felt a surge of frustration, mixed with concern. Rachel was trapped in a web of secrets, and I needed to free her.

As I left the kitchen, my mind reeling with questions, I spotted my brother, Julian, lingering in the foyer. His eyes, usually bright with amusement, seemed dulled, his expression guarded.

"Julian, what are you doing up so early?" I asked, my tone casual.

He shrugged, his shoulders barely rising. "Couldn't sleep. What's going on, Ava?"

I hesitated, unsure how much to reveal. "Just talking to Rachel about...family business."

Julian's gaze narrowed. "The embezzlement?"

I nodded, surprised. "How did you know?"

"I overheard Father talking to his lawyer," Julian said, his voice low.

I felt a pang of unease. Julian's involvement could complicate things.

"Do you know anything about it?" I asked, searching his face.

Julian shook his head. "No, but I think we should talk to Elijah."

"Elijah?" I repeated, my mind racing.

"Yeah, Father's business partner. He might know something."

I nodded, intrigued. Elijah Thompson was a mysterious figure, always lurking in the shadows.

As we walked toward the study, I noticed Julian's unease.

"Julian, what's bothering you?" I asked.

He hesitated, then spoke in a hushed tone. "I think Father's in trouble, Ava. Deep trouble."

My heart sank. Julian's words echoed my own fears.

"We'll figure it out," I reassured him.

But as we entered the study, I couldn't shake off the feeling that we were walking into a minefield.

CHAPTER THREE

As Julian and I entered the study, Elijah Thompson stood by the window, his gaze fixed on the city skyline, the morning light casting an ethereal glow on his chiseled features. His presence commanded attention, exuding an aura of power and sophistication that seemed almost palpable.

"Ava, Julian," he said, his voice smooth as silk, "I see you're both aware of the situation, though perhaps not fully cognizant of its far-reaching implications."

My father's eyes narrowed, his expression strained. "Elijah, what do you know about the embezzlement?"

Elijah's expression remained impassive, his piercing blue eyes glinting with a hint of secrets untold. "I know enough to say that this is more than just a financial issue, August. It's a matter of trust, of loyalty, and of the very foundations upon which Blackwood Industries was built."

Julian shifted uncomfortably, his eyes darting toward our father. "What do you mean?" he asked, his voice tinged with unease.

Elijah's gaze swept the room, his eyes lingering on each of us before responding. "Someone has compromised the very fabric of our organization, exploiting vulnerabilities and manipulating finances with alarming precision. We need to identify the culprit before it's too late, before the damage becomes irreparable."

My father's face paled, his eyes sunken with worry. "Elijah, I—"

"No, August," Elijah interrupted, his voice firm but measured. "We can't afford to sugarcoat this. The stakes are too high, the consequences too dire. We're facing a crisis of epic proportions, one that threatens to destroy everything we've built."

I sensed a hidden agenda behind Elijah's words, a subtle undercurrent that hinted at secrets and lies.

"What's at stake?" I pressed, my voice firm.

Elijah's eyes locked onto mine, his gaze piercing. "The future of Blackwood Industries, Ava. And perhaps...more."

As Elijah's words hung in the air, the tension in the room became palpable. My father's face seemed to crumble, his eyes sunken with worry.

"Ava, Julian," Elijah continued, his voice measured, "we're facing a crisis of epic proportions. The embezzlement is just the tip of the iceberg. There are whispers of insider trading, of corporate espionage, and of a mole within our organization."

Julian's eyes widened, his face pale. "That's impossible," he whispered.

Elijah's expression remained grim. "I'm afraid it's not. We've received intel suggesting that someone has been feeding sensitive information to our competitors. The consequences are catastrophic."

My mind reeled as I processed the information. Who could be behind this? And why?

"Elijah," I said, my voice firm, "we need to know more about the embezzlement. Who's involved? How much is at stake?"

Elijah nodded, his eyes locked onto mine. "The embezzlement amounts to tens of millions. As for who's involved...that's what we need to find out."

My father's voice was barely above a whisper. "Elijah, what if it's someone close to us?"

Elijah's expression turned grave. "August, we have to consider every possibility. We can't afford to rule out anyone."

The room fell silent, the weight of Elijah's words settling upon us like a physical force.

"Then we'll investigate everyone," Julian said, his voice resolute.

Elijah nodded. "I've already begun. But Ava, Julian, you must understand: this is a treacherous path we're walking. There will be secrets, lies, and betrayals. Are you prepared for that?"

I met Elijah's gaze, my heart pounding in anticipation.

"We're ready," I said.

CHAPTER FOUR

As Elijah's investigation unfolded, I found myself entangled in a web of deceit and secrets, each thread meticulously woven to conceal the truth. The cryptic message on the company's secure server - "Eclipse Initiative. Project Nightshade" - echoed in my mind, its significance tantalizingly out of reach.

"Ava, I need your expertise," Elijah said, his voice low and urgent, as we stood in the study surrounded by shelves lined with leather-bound tomes and the faint scent of old paper. "This message may be the key to unraveling the embezzlement, but I fear we're running out of time."

I nodded, my mind racing with possibilities. "What makes you think it's connected to Father's past?"

Elijah's expression turned somber. "A whisper in the dark, a rumor of a long-buried secret. Your father's involvement with the Eclipse Initiative may have far-reaching consequences."

Just then, Julian burst into the room, his eyes shining with excitement. "Ava, I found something!" he exclaimed.

"What is it?" I asked.

"A hidden safe in Father's office," Julian replied. "And inside...a letter addressed to you, sealed with a wax stamp bearing the Blackwood crest."

My hands trembled as I opened the letter, the words dancing on the page like a sinister waltz.

"Ava," the letter read, "if you're reading this, I'm in grave danger. Trust no one. Not even Elijah. The truth about your mother's death...it's not what you think."

My world shattered, the fragments of my reality scattered like autumn leaves in a gust of wind.

Just then, the door opened, and a woman with piercing green eyes and raven-black hair entered. "Ava, I'm Sophia Patel, Elijah's associate," she said.

I sensed a quiet strength in Sophia, a steeliness that belied her elegant demeanor.

"Sophia's expertise in forensic accounting will be invaluable," Elijah explained.

As Sophia delved into the financial records, her eyes scanned the pages with a practiced intensity, her brow furrowed in concentration. "Ava, I think I've found something," she said, her voice measured, "a series of transactions, hidden behind layers of shell companies, that point to a single entity: the Nightshade Corporation."

I felt a shiver run down my spine as Elijah's expression turned grim. "Nightshade is a ghost company, Ava," he explained. "No one knows who's behind it, but its involvement suggests a level of sophistication and deceit that goes far beyond simple embezzlement."

The room seemed to darken, as if the shadows themselves were closing in around us. I couldn't shake off the feeling that we were being manipulated, that every step we took was being orchestrated by an unseen hand.

"What's the connection between Nightshade and the Eclipse Initiative?" I asked, my voice barely above a whisper.

THE FAMILY OF DECEPTION

Sophia's eyes locked onto mine. "I'm not sure, but I think it's more than just a coincidence. The Eclipse Initiative seems to be a codename for a larger operation, one that involves multiple players and shell companies."

Elijah nodded. "We need to dig deeper. Ava, I want you to review your father's correspondence, see if there's any mention of Nightshade or the Eclipse Initiative."

As I nodded, Julian spoke up. "I'll start searching online, see if I can find any connections between Nightshade and other companies."

The silence that followed was oppressive, punctuated only by the soft hum of the computer and the rustle of papers.

Suddenly, Sophia's eyes widened. "Ava, I've found something," she exclaimed. "A hidden email account, linked to your father's name. The password is...your mother's name."

My heart skipped a beat. "Open it," I said, my voice firm.

The email inbox revealed a shocking message:

"Meet me at the old warehouse at midnight. Come alone. - J"

The message was dated the night before my mother's death.

CHAPTER FIVE

As I stared at the cryptic message on the screen, the words seemed to sear themselves into my brain, igniting a firestorm of questions and fears. Who was the mysterious sender, and what was the purpose of the clandestine meeting? And why, oh why, had my father kept this secret hidden for so long?

The room around me dissolved into a haze of uncertainty, leaving only the haunting memory of my mother's tragic death. Had her demise been more than just a tragic accident? Was it connected to this mysterious meeting?

Elijah's voice pierced the fog of my thoughts. "Ava, we need to investigate this further. We can't ignore the possibility that your father's involvement with Nightshade and the Eclipse Initiative led to your mother's death."

Sophia's eyes locked onto mine, her expression somber. "I'll dig deeper into the email trail, see if I can uncover any more clues."

Julian's face was set in determination. "I'll search for any connections between the old warehouse and Nightshade."

As the team sprang into action, I felt a sense of unease creeping over me. We were playing with fire, dancing on the edge of a volcano. What secrets would we uncover, and at what cost?

The hours ticked by like hours on a countdown timer, each one ramping up the tension. Midnight loomed before us, a specter of unknown dangers.

As we approached the old warehouse, the shadows seemed to deepen, the darkness coalescing into menacing forms. I felt a chill run down my spine.

"This is it," Elijah whispered, his eyes scanning the deserted alley. "The meeting place."

Suddenly, a figure emerged from the darkness.

The figure stepped forward, its features illuminated by the faint moonlight. I gasped, my heart racing with anticipation.

"Ava," the figure said, its voice low and husky.

"Who are you?" I demanded.

The figure hesitated, then pulled off its hood, revealing a woman with piercing green eyes.

"Samantha Jenkins," Elijah whispered. "Your father's former assistant."

Samantha's gaze locked onto mine. "Ava, I've been watching you. I know what you're looking for."

"What do you know about my mother's death?" I pressed.

Samantha's expression turned somber. "I know it was no accident. Your father...he was involved with Nightshade. He was in over his head."

Julian's eyes widened. "What do you mean?"

Samantha's voice dropped to a whisper. "Your father was blackmailing Nightshade. He had evidence of their wrongdoings, and he was using it to protect himself."

My mind reeled. Blackmail? My father?

Suddenly, footsteps echoed through the alley.

"We're not alone," Elijah warned.

Samantha's eyes darted around. "We have to get out of here. Now"

As we navigated the deserted alley, the shadows seemed to writhe and twist around us, like living darkness. The air was heavy with anticipation, each breath weighted with the promise of revelation.

Samantha Jenkins, my father's former assistant, walked alongside me, her piercing green eyes darting nervously around the alley. Her voice was barely above a whisper as she spoke.

"Ava, I've been watching you, waiting for the right moment to reveal the truth. Your father's involvement with Nightshade was far more sinister than you could have imagined."

I felt a shiver run down my spine as Elijah's eyes locked onto Samantha's. "What do you mean?" he asked.

Samantha's expression turned somber, her words dripping with conviction. "Your father was blackmailing Nightshade, using his knowledge of their illicit activities to protect himself and his family. But it was a precarious balancing act, and eventually, he fell prey to their machinations."

Julian's eyes widened in horror. "You're saying Nightshade killed our mother?"

Samantha's nod was almost imperceptible. "I'm saying they were involved. Your father's evidence was the key to unraveling their web of deceit, but it's gone now, lost in the depths of their corruption."

As we turned to leave, the sound of footsteps echoed through the alley, growing louder with each passing moment. Elijah's eyes narrowed.

"We're not alone," he warned.

THE FAMILY OF DECEPTION

A figure emerged from the shadows, its face obscured by a mask. The air seemed to vibrate with tension as Samantha's voice dropped to a whisper.

"Run."

As we sprinted through the alley, the mask-clad figure gave chase, its footsteps pounding the pavement in relentless pursuit. The darkness seemed to swirl around us, obscuring our path and heightening our fear.

Samantha's breathless voice guided us through the twisting alleys. "This way! We need to lose them."

We burst into a nearby parking garage, the sudden echo of our footsteps off the concrete walls disorienting. Elijah yanked open the door of a waiting car, ushering us inside.

As we sped away from the garage, the masked figure receded into the distance, but the sense of danger lingered. Julian's eyes locked onto Samantha.

"Who was that?" he demanded.

Samantha's expression turned grim. "Nightshade's enforcers. They'll stop at nothing to silence us."

I felt a chill run down my spine. "What did my father know?"

Samantha hesitated before speaking. "Your father discovered Nightshade's true purpose: manipulating global markets for their gain. He had evidence, documents and recordings, but it's gone now."

Elijah's eyes narrowed. "We need to find that evidence."

Samantha nodded. "I know where it might be hidden."

The car screeched to a halt before a dilapidated warehouse on the outskirts of town. Samantha's eyes locked onto mine.

"Are you ready, Ava?"

CHAPTER SIX

As we entered the dilapidated warehouse, the air thick with dust and decay, Samantha led us to a hidden room. "Your father's evidence is here," she said, her voice barely above a whisper.

Elijah's eyes scanned the space, his hand instinctively reaching for his gun. "Where?"

Samantha pointed to a concealed safe. "The combination is hidden in a fake rock outside."

Julian retrieved the rock, revealing the combination etched into its base. The safe creaked open, revealing stacks of documents, audio recordings, and a small notebook.

I felt a surge of hope. "This must be the proof we need."

Samantha nodded. "Your father documented everything: transactions, meetings, and names."

As we began to sift through the evidence, a shocking revelation emerged. The embezzlement was just the tip of the iceberg. Nightshade had infiltrated our company, manipulating finances and decisions.

Elijah's expression turned grim. "We need to take this to the authorities."

But as we prepared to leave, the sound of sirens pierced the air. The warehouse was surrounded.

"We have to get out of here, now," Elijah urged.

Samantha nodded. "There's a hidden exit. Follow me."

We sprinted through the warehouse, the sound of shattering glass and pounding footsteps closing in. The masked figures from the alley had found us.

Julian grasped my hand. "Stay close."

We burst through the hidden exit, emerging into a narrow alley. Samantha led us to a waiting van.

As we sped away, Elijah examined the evidence. "This is it. The proof we need to bring down Nightshade."

But my mind was racing with questions. Who was behind Nightshade? And what was their ultimate goal?

Suddenly, Sophia's voice crackled over the phone. "Elijah, I've hacked into Nightshade's server. I've found the embezzlement trail."

Elijah's eyes locked onto mine. "What does it lead to?"

Sophia's pause was ominous. "Your family's company. The embezzlement goes all the way to the top."

My world shattered. Could it be true? Was our family responsible for the embezzlement?

My mind reeled as Sophia's words hung in the air. Embezzlement within our family's company? It couldn't be true.

Elijah's expression turned grim. "We need to investigate further."

Samantha nodded. "I have access to the company's financial records. Let's review them."

As we poured over the documents, a disturbing pattern emerged. Large sums of money had been siphoned off, hidden behind layers of shell companies.

Julian's eyes widened. "This is massive. Millions of dollars."

I felt a wave of nausea. Our family's reputation, our legacy, was at stake.

Suddenly, Sophia's voice crackled over the phone again. "Elijah, I've found something. A transaction linked to your father's account."

My heart sank. Dad?

Elijah's eyes locked onto mine. "We need to confront him."

But as we arrived at my family's estate, a surprise awaited us. My father, standing in the foyer, a mix of anger and fear etched on his face.

"Ava, what's going on?" He demanded

"Ava, what's going on?" my father repeated, his voice firm but laced with unease.

I stood tall, my heart pounding. "We know about the embezzlement, Dad. We have evidence."

His expression faltered, and for a moment, I saw a glimmer of guilt. But then, his mask slipped back into place.

"I don't know what you're talking about," he said, his voice cold.

Elijah stepped forward. "Don't lie, sir. We have records of transactions linked to your account."

My father's eyes narrowed. "You're meddling in things you don't understand."

Samantha's voice was firm. "We understand enough to know you're involved with Nightshade."

The room fell silent, the tension palpable.

Suddenly, my father's demeanor changed. He seemed to deflate, his shoulders sagging.

"Fine," he whispered. "I'll tell you the truth."

CHAPTER SEVEN

My father's words hung in the air like a challenge. "I'll tell you the truth."

As my father's words hung in the air, the weight of his confession settled upon us like a physical burden. I felt my heart sink, my mind racing with the implications of his revelation.

"I was coerced into working with Nightshade," he repeated, his voice laced with desperation. "They threatened to harm your mother, Ava, if I didn't comply with their demands."

Elijah's eyes narrowed, his gaze piercing. "What exactly did they want you to do?" he pressed.

My father's voice cracked, the sound echoing through the room like a fragile vase shattering on stone. "I had to embezzle funds, launder money through our company, and provide them with access to our business network. I was trapped, caught in a web of deceit from which I couldn't escape."

Samantha's expression turned sympathetic, her eyes filled with compassion. "Why didn't you seek help?" she asked gently.

My father's eyes dropped, his gaze falling to the floor like a defeated man. "I was ashamed," he whispered. "And scared. Nightshade's reach is vast, their influence pervasive. I feared for our lives, for our family's safety."

Julian's voice was firm, resolute. "We need to take this to the authorities," he declared.

But my father's words stopped us cold, his warning echoing through the room like a death knell. "You can't," he said. "Nightshade has infiltrated every level of law enforcement, every branch of government. We're on our own, isolated and vulnerable."

My father's warning hung in the air, a dire prediction that seemed to suffocate us. I felt a chill run down my spine as I grasped the magnitude of Nightshade's influence.

"What do you mean they've infiltrated every level?" Elijah asked, his voice low and urgent.

My father's eyes darted nervously around the room. "They have moles in the police department, the FBI, even the government. If we go to the authorities, Nightshade will know. They'll silence us before we can expose them."

Samantha's expression turned grim. "We need to gather evidence, build a case against them."

Julian nodded. "But how can we trust anyone?"

My father's face twisted in anguish. "I'm sorry. I should have been stronger. I should have protected our family."

I took a step forward, my heart aching for my father. "We'll get through this together," I said.

But as I looked into his eyes, I saw a flicker of doubt. Was he telling us everything?

Suddenly, Sophia's voice crackled over the phone. "Elijah, I've hacked into Nightshade's server. I've found a cryptic message."

Elijah's eyes locked onto mine. "What does it say?"

Sophia's pause was ominous. "It says: 'Project Eclipse is activated. Targets acquired.'"

CHAPTER EIGHT

Sophia's words sent a shiver down my spine. "Project Eclipse? What does it mean?"

Elijah's eyes locked onto mine. "We need to find out."

Samantha nodded. "I'll dig into Nightshade's files. See if I can uncover any connections."

Julian's voice was firm. "We need to assume we're targets. We need to protect ourselves."

My father's face paled. "I've put you all in danger. I'm sorry."

I placed a reassuring hand on his shoulder. "We'll get through this together."

As we dispersed to gather information, my mind raced with questions. What was Project Eclipse? And why had Nightshade targeted us?

Hours passed, the tension building as we waited for Sophia's update.

Finally, her voice crackled over the phone. "Elijah, I've found something. Project Eclipse is a covert operation to eliminate potential threats to Nightshade's operations."

Elijah's eyes narrowed. "What kind of threats?"

Sophia's pause was ominous. "Whistleblowers, investigators, journalists... anyone who could expose Nightshade's crimes."

My heart sank. We were in grave danger.

Suddenly, the lights flickered, and the room plunged into darkness.

As we navigated the darkness, the oppressive silence threatened to suffocate us, heavy with an unsettling energy that seemed to seep into every pore. I strained my ears, listening intently for any sound that might indicate what was happening, my heart pounding in anticipation.

Suddenly, Elijah's voice cut through the silence, his tone calm and reassuring. "Everyone, stay calm. We need to assess the situation and determine our next move."

Samantha's voice was steady, her words punctuated by the soft glow of her phone's flashlight as she swept the beam across the room. "I've got my phone's light. Let me check the room for any signs of intrusion."

The beam of light sliced through the darkness, illuminating the space with an eerie glow. We were alone, but the air seemed to vibrate with tension, as if unseen eyes watched our every move.

Julian's voice was low and urgent, his words laced with a growing sense of unease. "We need to get out of here, now. We can't stay trapped in this darkness."

My father nodded, his face set in determination as he led us through the winding hallways. "I know a way out. Follow me."

We moved swiftly, our footsteps echoing through the darkened hallway like a death knell, the silence between us thick with unspoken fears. The creaking of old wooden floorboards beneath our feet seemed to reverberate through the stillness.

As we reached the exit, a sudden burst of light illuminated the night sky, casting long shadows across the lawn. The lights of the estate's security system flickered back to life, but something was off.

Elijah's eyes narrowed, his gaze scanning the perimeter. "That's not our security system. It's been hacked."

Samantha's voice was grim, her words barely above a whisper. "Nightshade's here. We're surrounded."

The words hung in the air like a death sentence. Nightshade's presence seemed to suffocate us, their sinister intentions palpable.

"We need to get out of here, now," Elijah urged, his voice low and urgent.

Samantha nodded, her eyes scanning the perimeter. "I'll check the gates. See if we can make a clean escape."

Julian's face was set in determination. "I'll cover our six. Make sure we're not followed."

My father's eyes locked onto mine. "Ava, stay close to me. We'll get through this together."

I nodded, my heart racing with fear. We moved swiftly, our footsteps echoing through the night air.

As we reached the gates, Samantha's voice was laced with tension. "We've got a problem. The gates are sealed. Nightshade's got us trapped."

Elijah's eyes narrowed. "Find another way out."

Samantha's fingers flew across her phone's screen. "I've got a possible route. Follow me."

We sprinted through the darkness, our breaths coming in ragged gasps. The night air seemed to vibrate with danger.

Suddenly, a figure emerged from the shadows.

CHAPTER NINE

As Aiden's menacing figure emerged from the darkness, the faint moonlight dancing across his features seemed to accentuate the sinister transformation that had taken hold of him, rendering the man who had once been my family's trusted ally almost unrecognizable. The warmth in his eyes, once a beacon of comfort, had been extinguished, replaced by an icy calculating gaze that sent shivers down my spine.

"Aiden?" I whispered, my voice trembling as I struggled to reconcile the man before me with the one I thought I knew.

The sound of my voice seemed to trigger a cruel smile, his lips twisting into a malevolent grin. "You shouldn't have dug so deep, Ava," he said, his voice dripping with malice, each word laced with a sinister intent that made my skin crawl.

Elijah stepped forward, his gun drawn, the movement fluid and deliberate, a clear warning to Aiden to keep his distance. "You're with Nightshade," Elijah stated, his tone firm, leaving no room for doubt.

Aiden's smile broadened, his eyes glinting with amusement. "I'm whatever they need me to be," he replied, his voice devoid of emotion, his words echoing with a chilling detachment.

Samantha's eyes narrowed, her gaze piercing as she studied Aiden's demeanor. "What do you want, Aiden?" she asked, her voice firm, her words measured.

He took a step closer, his movements fluid and menacing, his presence seeming to fill the space around us. "I want what you're looking for," he said, his voice low, his words dripping with menace. "The evidence. Hand it over, and I might let you live."

Julian's voice was firm, resolute. "We'll never give it to you," he declared, his words a clear defiance against Aiden's threats.

Aiden chuckled, the sound sending shivers down my spine. "You don't understand the game you're playing," he said, his voice dripping with condescension. "Nightshade always wins."

As Aiden's words hung in the air like a specter, his smile twisting into a cruel grin, Elijah's grip on his gun tightened, his eyes narrowing with a mixture of suspicion and determination. "Who's behind Nightshade?" he demanded, his voice firm and resolute.

Aiden chuckled, the sound low and menacing, his eyes glinting with amusement. "You'll never touch the architects," he said, his voice dripping with condescension. "They're ghosts, invisible and untouchable, their identities hidden behind a web of deceit and corruption."

Samantha's eyes narrowed, her gaze piercing as she studied Aiden's demeanor. "What's their endgame?" she asked, her voice measured and deliberate.

Aiden's gaze flicked to hers, his expression unreadable. "Control," he replied, his voice devoid of emotion. "Power. The ability to shape the world to their design, bending the rules to suit their interests, crushing anyone who dares to oppose them."

Julian's voice was firm, resolute. "We won't let that happen," he declared, his words a clear defiance against Nightshade's sinister plans.

Aiden shrugged, his shoulders barely rising off the ground. "You're no match for Nightshade's resources," he said, his voice dripping with malice. "They'll crush you, annihilate you, leaving nothing but ashes in their wake."

Suddenly, a faint hum filled the air, growing louder, the sound of engines roaring to life. Headlights illuminated the darkness, casting long shadows across the ground.

A black SUV screeched to a halt beside us, the door sliding open with a soft whoosh. A woman with piercing green eyes stepped out, her gaze locking onto mine.

"Welcome, Ava," she said, her voice dripping with sophistication, her smile icy and calculated. "I've been waiting. My name is Nadia Petrov. I'm Nightshade's CEO, the architect of your downfall."

CHAPTER TEN

Nadia Petrov's gaze locked onto mine, her piercing green eyes seeming to bore into my soul with an unnerving intensity that sent shivers down my spine. "Ava, you're a remarkable woman," she said, her voice dripping with sincerity, each word carefully crafted to convey a sense of genuine admiration.

Elijah's eyes narrowed, his brow furrowed in suspicion as he stepped forward, his movements fluid and deliberate. "What do you want, Nadia?" he demanded, his voice firm and resolute.

Nadia's smile widened, her lips curving upward in a calculated gesture that seemed to mask a deeper motive. "I want to offer Ava a choice," she said, her voice measured and deliberate. "Join Nightshade, and we'll spare your family's lives, ensuring their safety and well-being. Refuse, and... well, let's just say we have measures in place to ensure cooperation, measures that will make your worst nightmares seem tame by comparison."

Samantha's voice was firm, her words laced with determination. "Ava will never join you," she declared, her eyes flashing with defiance.

Nadia chuckled, the sound low and menacing, her gaze never wavering from mine. "We'll see about that," she said, her voice dripping with confidence. "Ava, you see, has something we need, something that could change the course of history, something that will give us the upper hand in a world where power is everything."

Julian's eyes locked onto Nadia, his expression skeptical. "What are you talking about?" he asked, his voice firm.

Nadia's gaze never wavered. "The Eclipse File," she replied, her voice devoid of emotion. "We know your father had it. We know Ava's been searching for it. And we'll stop at nothing to get it, no matter the cost, no matter the consequences."

Aiden stepped forward, his eyes cold and calculating. "You have 24 hours to decide, Ava," he said, his voice devoid of emotion. "After that... consequences will be severe, consequences that will destroy everything you hold dear."

Nadia's twisted smile lingered, etched in my memory like a scar. "Consequences you can't even imagine," she whispered, her voice dripping with malice.

Elijah's eyes blazed with determination. "We'll never give in," he declared.

Nadia chuckled, the sound sending shivers down my spine. "We'll see about that," she said, her gaze flicking to Aiden. "Ensure Ava understands the gravity of her decision."

Aiden nodded, his eyes cold. "You have 24 hours, Ava. After that, Nightshade's agents will extract the Eclipse File by any means necessary."

Samantha's voice trembled with rage. "You'll never get away with this."

Nadia's smile widened. "Oh, but we already have. We've infiltrated every aspect of your lives. Your family's business, your personal relationships... we know everything."

Julian's face paled. "What do you want with the Eclipse File?"

Nadia's gaze locked onto mine, her eyes piercing with an unnerving intensity. "The Eclipse File holds the key to unlocking Nightshade's true potential," she said, her voice dripping with conviction. "With it, we'll control the global economy, manipulate world events... and reshape the world in our image."

The weight of Nadia's words crushed me. Could I really risk everything to stop Nightshade? The thought sent a chill down my spine.

Elijah's voice cut through the tension. "You're insane, Nadia. You'll never get away with this."

Nadia's smile twisted. "Oh, but we already have," she said, her voice laced with malice. "We've infiltrated every aspect of your lives. Your family's business, your personal relationships... we know everything."

Samantha's eyes blazed with determination. "We'll expose you," she vowed.

Nadia chuckled. "Try. But you'll find that our reach is far greater than you ever imagined."

Suddenly, Aiden stepped forward, his eyes cold. "Time's running out, Ava. You have 23 hours and 59 minutes to decide."

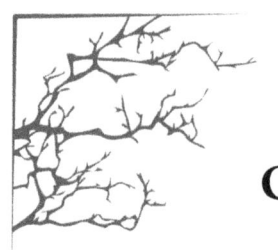

CHAPTER ELEVEN

The countdown had begun, and I felt like I was trapped in a suffocating nightmare, with the weight of Nightshade's ultimatum crushing me. 23 hours and 59 minutes to decide: join the organization or risk everything I held dear.

Elijah's eyes locked onto mine, his expression resolute, his jaw set in determination. "We'll figure this out, Ava," he vowed, his voice firm and reassuring. "We won't let Nightshade win, no matter what it takes."

Samantha nodded, her voice firm, her words laced with conviction. "We'll find a way to expose Nightshade, to bring them down and shatter their grip on our lives."

Julian's face was set in determination, his eyes burning with resolve. "We'll protect you, Ava," he promised. "No matter what Nightshade throws at us, we'll stand strong, united."

But I knew the truth, the harsh reality that threatened to consume me. Nightshade was a monster, a hydra-like organization that would stop at nothing to achieve its goals.

Nadia's smile lingered in my mind, her eyes piercing with malice, her voice whispering sinister sweet nothings in my thoughts. "You'll never win," she taunted. "Nightshade will always be one step ahead."

THE FAMILY OF DECEPTION 37

I pushed the darkness away, focusing on the task at hand, my mind racing with possibilities. "We need to gather evidence," I said, my voice firm, my words measured. "Something concrete to take down Nightshade, to expose their corruption and deceit."

Elijah nodded, his eyes locked onto mine. "I'll hack into their system, dig deep into their digital trail," he said, his voice filled with determination.

Samantha's eyes sparkled, her face set in resolve. "I'll dig into their financials, follow the money trail," she vowed.

Julian's face set in determination. "I'll investigate their operations, find the weak link in their chain," he promised.

Together, we formed a plan, racing against the clock, our hearts pounding with anticipation.

But Nightshade was always one step ahead, waiting in the shadows, ready to strike.

As we worked tirelessly to gather evidence, the clock ticked away with relentless precision, each passing minute bringing us closer to the daunting deadline that loomed over us like a specter. 22 hours and 14 minutes remained, a shrinking window of opportunity that threatened to slam shut at any moment.

Elijah's fingers flew across his keyboard with lightning speed, his eyes fixed intently on the screen as he navigated the complex digital landscape. "I've got something," he muttered, his voice barely audible over the hum of the computer.

Samantha leaned in, her eyes scanning the data with rapt attention, her brow furrowed in concentration. "What is it?" she asked, her voice laced with anticipation.

Elijah's face lit up with excitement, his eyes sparkling with triumph. "A hidden server," he announced, his voice filled with pride. "Nightshade's using it to coordinate their operations, to pull the strings from behind the scenes."

Julian's eyes narrowed, his gaze piercing as he scrutinized the information. "Can we access it?" he asked, his voice firm and resolute.

Elijah nodded, his confidence growing. "I'm working on it," he said, his fingers dancing across the keyboard with renewed urgency.

I paced the room, my mind racing with possibilities, my heart pounding in my chest like a drum. "We need concrete evidence," I stressed, my voice firm and determined. "Something to take to the authorities, something that will bring Nightshade crashing down."

Samantha's voice was firm, her words laced with conviction. "We'll get it, Ava," she vowed. "We won't let Nightshade win, no matter what it takes."

But doubts crept in, whispering insidious doubts in my ear, sowing seeds of fear and uncertainty. What if we failed? What if Nightshade silenced us forever, burying the truth beneath a shroud of secrecy and deceit?

Suddenly, Elijah's eyes snapped up, his face frozen in shock, his eyes wide with horror. "What is it?" I whispered, my heart skipping a beat.

Elijah's voice trembled, his words barely audible. "It's worse than we thought," he stammered. "Nightshade's planned something big, something that will change everything."

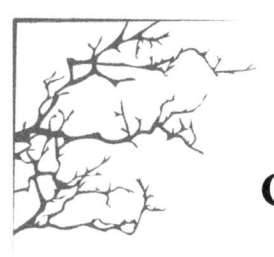

CHAPTER TWELVE

Elijah's revelation hung in the air like a ticking time bomb, threatening to shatter the fragile facade of our reality, to expose the dark underbelly of corruption and deceit that lurked beneath the surface of Nightshade's sinister operations. Nightshade's infiltration of the government was a cancer, spreading its dark tendrils through the highest echelons of power, insidiously manipulating policy to suit their nefarious agenda.

Samantha's eyes blazed with determination, her jaw set in a resolute mask. "We need to expose them," she vowed, her voice firm and unwavering, "to bring them down and shatter their grip on our lives."

Julian's face set in a similarly resolute expression. "We'll need concrete evidence," he cautioned, his voice measured and deliberate, "something that will stand up to scrutiny and bring Nightshade to its knees."

I nodded, my mind racing with the implications, my thoughts consumed by the sheer magnitude of Nightshade's betrayal. "Elijah, can you dig deeper?" I asked, my voice barely above a whisper.

Elijah's fingers flew across his keyboard, his eyes locked onto the screen with laser-like intensity. "I'm trying," he muttered, his voice barely audible over the hum of the computer, "but Nightshade's security is like Fort Knox, impenetrable and unforgiving."

Suddenly, his eyes snapped up, a look of triumph flashing across his face. "I've got something," he exclaimed, his voice filled with excitement.

We gathered around him, our hearts pounding in unison, our anticipation building to a fever pitch.

"What is it?" I asked, my voice barely above a whisper.

Elijah's face was grim. "A memo from Nightshade's CEO, Nadia Petrov," he revealed, his voice laced with trepidation. "It mentions a project codenamed 'Eclipse.'"

The room fell silent, the weight of Elijah's words crushing us, the implications hanging in the air like a guillotine.

"What does it mean?" Samantha asked, her voice laced with fear.

I knew. I knew exactly what it meant.

"Eclipse is more than just a project," I said, my voice firm. "It's a catastrophic event, one that will change the course of history, leaving destruction and chaos in its wake."

As the weight of Elijah's words settled upon us, the room seemed to shrink, the air thickening with tension. Samantha's eyes locked onto mine, her gaze searching for answers.

"What does Eclipse mean?" she asked, her voice barely above a whisper.

I hesitated, unsure how much to reveal. But Elijah's discovery changed everything.

"Eclipse is a codename," I began, my voice measured. "It represents a catastrophic event, one that will reshape the global landscape."

Julian's face paled. "What kind of event?"

I took a deep breath. "A financial collapse, orchestrated by Nightshade to gain control over the world's economy."

Samantha's eyes widened. "That's impossible."

I shook my head. "Not for Nightshade. They've infiltrated every level of government and finance. They have the resources and expertise to pull it off."

Elijah's face set in determination. "We can't let them."

I nodded. "We won't. But we need proof."

Julian's eyes narrowed. "And we need a plan."

As we began brainstorming, the clock ticked away, each passing minute bringing us closer to the deadline.

Suddenly, Elijah's phone buzzed. "It's an encrypted message," he said, his eyes scanning the screen.

"From who?" Samantha asked.

Elijah's face was grim. "Nadia Petrov."

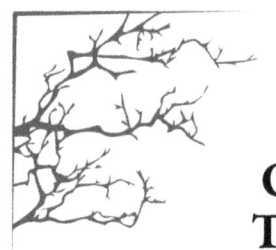

CHAPTER THIRTEEN

As Elijah's eyes scanned the encrypted message from Nadia Petrov, his expression transformed from determination to alarm, his face pale and tense. "It's a warning," he muttered, his voice barely audible over the hum of the computer.

Samantha's eyes locked onto Elijah's, her gaze searching for answers. "What kind of warning?" she asked, her voice laced with concern.

Elijah hesitated, his eyes darting between us. "Nadia knows we're onto Eclipse," he revealed. "She's threatening to take drastic measures if we don't back off."

Julian's face set in a resolute mask. "We can't back down now," he vowed. "We're too close to the truth."

I nodded, my mind racing with the implications. "We need to assume Nadia will stop at nothing to protect Eclipse," I said. "We must be prepared for anything."

As we strategized, the shadows in the room seemed to deepen, as if the darkness itself was closing in around us. Suddenly, Elijah's phone buzzed again.

"What is it?" Samantha asked.

Elijah's face was grim. "A text from an unknown number," he replied. "It says: 'Meet me at the old warehouse at midnight. Come alone.'"

The room fell silent, the weight of the message hanging in the air like a challenge.

The words "Come alone" echoed in my mind, a sinister whisper that sent shivers down my spine. Who was this mysterious messenger, and what did they want?

Samantha's voice broke the silence. "We can't trust this," she warned. "It's probably a trap."

Julian nodded. "Agreed. We should ignore it."

But something about the message resonated with me. A gut feeling that this was more than just a trap.

"I'll go," I said, my voice firm.

Elijah's eyes widened. "Ava, no!"

I stood up, my mind made up. "I have to know what this is about."

Samantha's face set in determination. "We'll come with you."

Julian nodded. "We're in this together."

I shook my head. "This time, I have to go alone."

The room fell silent, the tension between us palpable.

As I walked out into the night, the darkness seemed to swallow me whole. I felt like I was walking into a void, unsure what lay ahead.

The old warehouse loomed before me, its abandoned facade a haunting reminder of the secrets it held.

I took a deep breath and stepped inside.

As I stepped into the abandoned warehouse, the creaking of the old wooden floorboards beneath my feet echoed through the desolate space, sending shivers down my spine. The dim moonlight filtering through the grimy windows cast eerie shadows on the walls, making me feel like I was walking into a nightmare.

The air was thick with the scent of decay and neglect, and I couldn't shake the feeling that I was being watched. Every step I took seemed to reverberate through the silence, as if I was being herded towards some unknown fate.

Suddenly, a figure emerged from the darkness, its presence announced by the soft rustling of fabric. My heart skipped a beat as the figure stepped closer, its features obscured by the shadows.

"Who are you?" I demanded, trying to keep my voice steady.

The figure didn't respond, instead pulling out a small device from its pocket. The device emitted a soft hum, and a holographic image flickered to life before me.

I gasped as I recognized the image: Eclipse's logo, emblazoned on a screen filled with cryptic codes and symbols.

"What does this mean?" I asked, my mind racing.

The figure remained silent, its gaze fixed on me with an unnerving intensity.

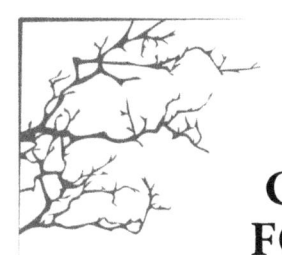

CHAPTER FOURTEEN

The figure's silence was deafening, its gaze piercing through me like a knife. I felt exposed, vulnerable, as if my very soul was being dissected.

Suddenly, the device's hum ceased, and the holographic image vanished. The figure turned to leave.

"Wait!" I called out, my voice echoing through the warehouse.

The figure paused, its back still turned.

"What do you want from me?" I demanded.

Slowly, the figure turned, its features still shrouded in shadows.

"You're getting close to the truth," it said, its voice distorted.

"About Eclipse?" I asked.

The figure nodded.

"What is it?" I pressed.

The figure hesitated, then handed me a small USB drive.

"Proof," it said. "But be warned: once you see this, there's no going back."

With that, the figure vanished into the darkness, leaving me stunned.

As I stood transfixed, my eyes scanning the revelations unfolding on my phone's screen, the darkness surrounding me seemed to grow thicker, like a palpable entity that threatened to suffocate me with its crushing weight. The files, meticulously compiled and cryptically labeled, revealed a labyrinthine network of deceit and corruption that stretched far beyond the confines of Nightshade's organization, ensnaring government agencies, corporations, and individuals in its sinister grasp.

Each new revelation struck me with the force of a hammer blow, shaking the very foundations of my understanding and leaving me reeling. Eclipse, the codename that had haunted my every waking moment, was more than just a project – it was a blueprint for global domination, a catastrophic event that would reshape the world in Nightshade's image.

My mind racing with the implications, I struggled to comprehend the sheer scale of Nightshade's ambition. Their tentacles reached into every level of society, manipulating and coercing with ruthless efficiency, leaving no stone unturned in their quest for absolute power.

The phone's screen seemed to blur before my eyes as the truth hit me like a tidal wave. I was no longer just fighting for my family's survival; I was fighting for humanity's very future.

Suddenly, my phone buzzed again, shrill and insistent, shattering the silence like a scream. I hesitated, unsure whether to answer, but something about the caller ID made my heart skip a beat – it was Elijah.

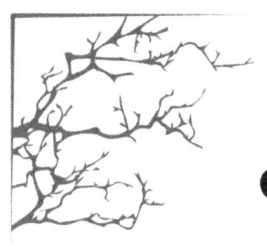

CHAPTER FIFTEEN

"Elijah, where are you?" I asked, my voice laced with urgency.

"I'm outside Nightshade's HQ," he replied, his tone low and cautious. "I managed to hack their security feed. Ava, you need to see this."

My heart racing, I asked, "What is it?"

"Eclipse's launch sequence has begun," Elijah said. "We have less than an hour before it's too late."

I felt like I'd been punched in the gut. "What can we do?"

"I'm working on disabling their servers," Elijah said. "But I need your help. Meet me at the east entrance."

Without hesitation, I agreed and ended the call. I knew the risks were mounting, but I was willing to take them.

I sprinted through the city streets, my heart pounding in my chest like a drum. The east entrance of Nightshade's HQ loomed before me, its sleek glass facade gleaming like a fortress.

As I approached, Elijah emerged from the shadows, his eyes locked on mine with a fierce intensity. "Ava, we're running out of time," he whispered, grasping my arm.

Together, we dashed into the building, dodging security guards and cameras with a precision that belied our desperation.

Elijah led the way, his knowledge of the layout guiding us through the maze-like corridors.

We reached the server room, a vast chamber humming with rows of computers. Elijah's fingers flew across the keyboard, his eyes racing with concentration.

"What's the plan?" I asked, my voice barely above a whisper.

"I'll create a virus to disable their systems," Elijah replied. "But we need to upload it to the mainframe."

Suddenly, alarms blared, and the lights flickered. Nightshade's security team had detected our presence.

"We're out of time," Elijah shouted, his fingers typing furiously.

With seconds to spare, he uploaded the virus. The computers around us began to crash, their screens freezing in a chaotic dance.

But our victory was short-lived. A figure emerged from the shadows, eyes blazing with fury.

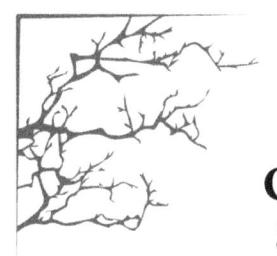

CHAPTER SIXTEEN

As the figure emerged from the shadows, its features illuminated by the flickering fluorescent lights, I felt a jolt of adrenaline course through my veins, my heart racing with anticipation. The air was electric with tension, the silence between us thick with unspoken threats.

"Ava, Elijah, you're meddling in affairs beyond your control," the figure growled, its voice low and menacing, echoing off the server room's walls.

I stood tall, my eyes locked on the figure, my mind racing with calculations. "We won't back down," I declared, my voice steady.

Elijah stepped forward, his eyes flashing with defiance. "We know what Nightshade's planning," he said. "And we'll stop it, no matter what."

The figure sneered, its lips curling into a cruel smile. "You're no match for Nightshade's resources," it taunted. "Eclipse will launch, and you'll be powerless to stop it."

With each passing second, the stakes escalated, the clock ticking away like a time bomb. I knew we had to act fast.

Suddenly, Elijah's eyes widened. "Ava, the virus – it's spreading," he whispered.

I turned to him, hope surging through me. "Can it stop Eclipse?"

Elijah nodded. "If we can reach the mainframe, yes."

We sprinted through the corridors, dodging Nightshade agents with a precision born of desperation. Elijah's eyes were fixed on his phone, tracking the virus's progress.

"We're close," he whispered, his voice urgent. "The mainframe is within reach."

I nodded, my heart racing. "Let's move."

We burst into the mainframe room, rows of servers humming before us. Elijah's fingers flew across the keyboard, his eyes locked on the screen.

"Almost there," he muttered.

Suddenly, the lights flickered, and the servers went dark. Nightshade's security team had initiated a shutdown.

"No!" Elijah shouted, frustration etched on his face.

But I saw an opportunity. "The backup systems," I whispered. "Can you access them?"

Elijah's eyes widened. "Yes, if I can bypass the encryption."

With seconds ticking away, Elijah worked his magic. The screens flickered back to life, and the mainframe's defenses began to crumble.

"We're in," Elijah breathed.

I smiled grimly. "Time to stop Eclipse."

CHAPTER SEVENTEEN

As we delved deeper into the mainframe, the digital landscape unfolding before us like a complex tapestry, Elijah's fingers danced across the keyboard with a precision that belied the desperation creeping into his eyes. The clock was ticking, each passing second bringing Eclipse closer to launch.

"We're navigating through their internal systems now," Elijah whispered, his voice barely audible over the hum of the servers. "If we can find the launch sequence, we might be able to—"

Suddenly, the screens flickered, and a warning message flashed before us: "Unauthorized Access Detected. Security Protocols Engaged."

My heart sank. "We've triggered their intrusion detection," I warned.

Elijah's eyes locked onto mine, a fierce determination burning within them. "We can't give up now," he urged. "We're too close."

With a deep breath, he launched into a frenzied typing spree, racing against the clock to outmaneuver Nightshade's security measures. The air was electric with tension, each passing moment heightening the stakes.

As the seconds ticked away, the silence between us grew thicker, punctuated only by the staccato beat of Elijah's fingers on the keyboard. And then, in a burst of triumph, he shouted, "I've got it! The launch sequence is—"

But his words were cut short by the sound of alarms blaring, and the lights flickering ominously.

The alarms grew louder, and the lights flickered wildly, casting eerie shadows on the walls. Elijah's eyes locked onto mine, his face set in a determined mask.

"We have to shut down the launch sequence," he shouted above the din.

I nodded, my heart racing. "How much time do we have?"

Elijah's gaze darted to the countdown timer on the screen. "Less than five minutes."

With a deep breath, he launched into a frenzied typing spree, racing against the clock to outmaneuver Nightshade's security measures. The air was electric with tension, each passing moment heightening the stakes.

As the seconds ticked away, the silence between us grew thicker, punctuated only by the staccato beat of Elijah's fingers on the keyboard. Sweat dripped from his brow, and his eyes blazed with focus.

Suddenly, the screens flickered, and a message flashed before us: "Launch Sequence Terminated. Eclipse Aborted."

Elijah's face lit up with triumph. "We did it!"

But our victory was short-lived. The alarms ceased, and the lights stabilized, revealing a figure standing in the doorway, eyes blazing with fury.

"Congratulations, Ava," the figure sneered. "You've just sealed your fate."

THE FAMILY OF DECEPTION

The figure's eyes blazed with fury, its gaze piercing through me like a dagger. "You think you've won, Ava," it sneered, "but you've only unleashed a catastrophe."

Elijah stepped forward, his face set in a defiant mask. "We'll never let you launch Eclipse," he declared.

The figure's smile twisted into a grotesque grin. "Eclipse is just the beginning," it said. "You've triggered a chain reaction, Ava. Nightshade's allies will ensure its launch, no matter what."

My mind reeled as the implications sank in. We'd played into Nightshade's hands, unleashing a global catastrophe.

Suddenly, the room erupted into chaos. Agents stormed in, surrounding us. The figure vanished into the fray, leaving us to face the consequences.

"Elijah, we have to get out!" I shouted.

He nodded, grabbing my hand. "Follow me!"

We sprinted through the corridors, pursued by Nightshade's agents. The stakes had never been higher.

As we burst into the night air, the city's neon lights blurred around us. We'd escaped, but for how long?

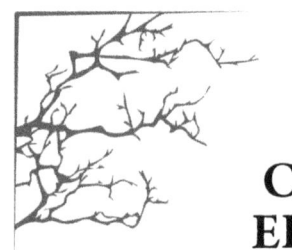

CHAPTER EIGHTEEN

As we sprinted through the city streets, the neon lights blurring around us like a kaleidoscope of colors, I felt the weight of our predicament settling in, the consequences of our actions unfolding like a complex tapestry. We'd stopped Eclipse, but at what cost? The city's nightlife, once a vibrant and pulsating entity, now seemed menacing, its shadows hiding unknown dangers.

Elijah's grip on my hand tightened, his fingers intertwining with mine in a reassuring gesture. "We need to find a safe house," he shouted above the din, his voice carrying a sense of urgency. "Somewhere Nightshade can't track us."

I nodded, my mind racing with the implications. Who could we trust? The city's underworld was a labyrinthine network of allegiances and rivalries, where loyalty was a luxury few could afford.

Suddenly, Elijah's phone buzzed, the screen illuminating his face with an otherworldly glow. He glanced at the message, his eyes narrowing as he processed the information.

"What is it?" I asked, my curiosity piqued.

"It's an unknown number," Elijah replied, his voice measured. "But the message... it's from someone claiming to be an ally.

They're offering us a safe haven, and information about Nightshade's plans."

My heart skipped a beat. Could this be our chance to turn the tables? I studied Elijah's face, searching for any sign of doubt or hesitation.

"What do you think?" I asked.

Elijah's gaze locked onto mine. "I think we have no choice," he said. "We need to take the risk."

With that, he typed out a response, his fingers flying across the keyboard. The silence that followed was oppressive, punctuated only by the distant hum of the city.

Then, Elijah's phone buzzed again. "It's the ally," he whispered. "They're sending us coordinates. We need to meet them within the hour."

I nodded, my heart racing with anticipation. Would this mysterious ally prove to be our salvation, or our downfall?

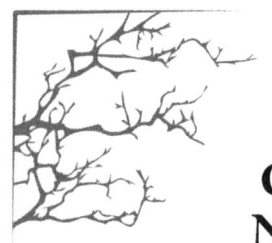

CHAPTER NINETEEN

We arrived at the designated location, a nondescript warehouse on the outskirts of the city. The ally's instructions were cryptic, but Elijah's determination was unwavering.

"This is it," he whispered, eyes scanning the perimeter. "Our only chance to take down Nightshade."

I nodded, heart racing. What lay ahead?

As we entered the warehouse, a figure emerged from the shadows. Tall, imposing, with eyes that seemed to bore into our souls.

"Welcome, Ava and Elijah," the figure said, voice low and gravelly. "I'm Phoenix. Your ally."

Phoenix's gaze swept over us, assessing our resolve. "Nightshade's plans are more complex than you imagine. Eclipse was merely a test run."

My mind reeled. "What do you mean?"

Phoenix's expression turned grim. "Nightshade's true goal is global domination. And you two are the only ones who can stop them."

Elijah's eyes narrowed. "How do we trust you?"

Phoenix smiled, a cold, calculated smile. "You don't. But you have no choice. I'm your only hope."

THE FAMILY OF DECEPTION

As Phoenix's words hung in the air, heavy with the weight of their ominous implications, I felt a shiver run down my spine, my mind racing to comprehend the sheer scope and complexity of Nightshade's far-reaching ambitions, which now loomed before us like an insurmountable behemoth, casting a dark shadow over the world.

"We've grossly underestimated Nightshade's reach and influence," Elijah whispered, his eyes locked onto Phoenix's, searching for any sign of deception or hidden motives, his gaze probing the depths of Phoenix's expression.

Phoenix nodded, his face set in a grim mask, his voice low and measured. "Nightshade's tentacles stretch far and wide, infiltrating governments, corporations, and institutions, quietly gathering power and manipulating events from the shadows, waiting for the perfect moment to strike and unleash their full fury upon the world."

I swallowed hard, the stark reality of our situation sinking in, the weight of our responsibility settling heavy on my shoulders. "And Eclipse was just a test run," I repeated, my voice barely above a whisper, the words echoing in my mind like a dire warning.

Phoenix's gaze turned intense, his eyes burning with a fierce determination. "A trial by fire, designed to gauge the world's response, to test the waters and identify potential threats, and now that they've succeeded, they'll stop at nothing to achieve their goal, no matter the cost in lives or destruction."

Elijah's jaw clenched, determination etched on his face, his voice firm and resolute. "We can't let that happen, Phoenix. We have to stop them, no matter what it takes."

Phoenix's smile was cold, calculated, and tinged with a hint of steel. "I've been gathering intelligence, waiting for the right moment to strike, and with your help, we can bring Nightshade down, but it won't be easy, and we'll have to be willing to take risks and face the consequences."

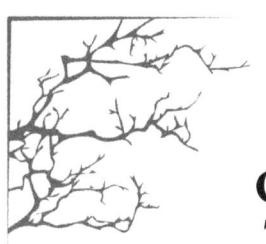

CHAPTER TWENTY

We stood at the entrance of Nightshade's headquarters, a towering skyscraper shrouded in darkness, its sleek glass façade reflecting the city's twinkling lights like a cold, unforgiving mirror. Phoenix's plan was set in motion, and our roles were clear, each of us aware of the daunting tasks that lay ahead.

"Elijah, hack into their mainframe and disable their security protocols," Phoenix whispered, his eyes scanning the perimeter with a practiced intensity. "Ava, take out their security team, using stealth and precision to minimize collateral damage. I'll handle the CEO, and ensure that Nightshade's sinister plans are brought to light."

My heart pounded in my chest as I nodded, my mind racing with the weight of our mission. This was it – our last stand against the forces of darkness that had haunted us for so long.

We moved swiftly, our actions synchronized with the precision of a well-oiled machine. Elijah's fingers flew across his keyboard, his eyes fixed on the screen as he navigated the labyrinthine digital landscape. Meanwhile, I slipped into the shadows, using my training to take down guards with silent efficiency.

Phoenix disappeared into the CEO's office, leaving us to our tasks, and the silence that followed was oppressive, punctuated only by the hum of computers and the occasional guard's cry. The air was thick with tension, heavy with the knowledge that our actions would determine the fate of countless lives.

Suddenly, Elijah's voice crackled through the comms device, his words laced with urgency. "Ava, I've got the mainframe access, but Nightshade's got a surprise waiting for us – a failsafe protocol that'll destroy all evidence and eliminate any witnesses."

My gut twisted with anxiety as I processed the implications. What now? Could we still stop Nightshade, or had we already lost?

"Phoenix is trapped," Elijah warned, his voice low and urgent. "We need to move, fast – every second counts."

As Elijah's urgent warning echoed through the comms device, I felt a surge of adrenaline coursing through my veins, propelling me into action with a renewed sense of purpose. With every passing second, the stakes grew higher, the consequences of failure looming larger than ever before.

"Phoenix is trapped, and we need to move, fast – every second counts," Elijah reiterated, his voice low and urgent, each word dripping with a sense of desperation. "We can't let Nightshade's CEO escape, not now that we've come so far."

I nodded to myself, my mind racing with the implications of Elijah's words. The CEO held the key to unlocking Nightshade's sinister plans, and if we failed to apprehend him, the consequences would be catastrophic.

With a deep breath, I sprang into action, my feet pounding the floor as I sprinted towards the CEO's office. The corridors blurred around me, a kaleidoscope of colors and sounds that faded into the background as I focused on my mission.

As I approached the office door, I could feel my heart pounding in my chest, my senses heightened as I prepared for the unknown dangers that lay ahead. The door swung open, revealing a scene of chaos and destruction.

Phoenix was pinned to the floor, Nightshade's CEO standing over him, a triumphant smile spreading across his face. "You'll never stop us," he sneered, his eyes flashing with malevolence.

With a fierce determination, I launched myself at the CEO, tackling him to the ground. Phoenix took advantage of the distraction to break free, his eyes flashing with gratitude.

"Thanks, Ava," he whispered, helping me pin the CEO down.

Elijah burst into the room, his face set in a triumphant smile. "I've disabled the failsafe protocol," he announced. "Nightshade's plans are ruined."

The CEO's face contorted with rage, but I held him firm, my grip unyielding. "It's over," I said, my voice cold and detached. "Your sinister plans will never come to fruition."

As the reality of their defeat sank in, the CEO's expression crumpled, revealing a depth of desperation and despair. "You'll never understand," he whispered, his voice barely audible. "We were trying to create a better world."

Phoenix's eyes narrowed. "By manipulating and controlling people? No, that's not a better world."

The CEO's gaze faltered, his eyes dropping to the floor. "I was blinded by ambition," he muttered. "I didn't see the harm."

Elijah's voice was firm. "You saw it. You just chose to ignore it."

As the truth dawned on the CEO, his face crumpled, overcome by the weight of his actions.

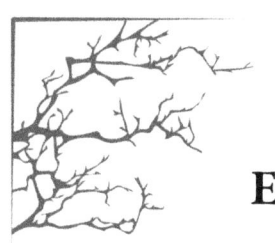

EPILOGUE

Six months had passed since Nightshade's downfall. Elijah and I had testified against the CEO, ensuring his imprisonment. Phoenix had vanished, his mission accomplished.

As I stood on the rooftop, gazing out at the city's twinkling lights, I felt a sense of closure. The darkness that had haunted me for so long was finally vanquished.

Elijah joined me, his hand finding mine. "You're free, Ava," he whispered.

I smiled, my heart full. "We're free."

Together, we looked out at the city, a new beginning unfolding before us.

But as I glanced at Elijah, I saw a hint of concern in his eyes. "What is it?" I asked.

"Phoenix," he replied. "I've been tracking his movements. He's not done yet."

My heart skipped a beat. "What do you mean?"

Elijah's expression turned serious. "Phoenix has a new target. One that could change everything."

I frowned, my mind racing. "What's the target?"

Elijah's eyes locked onto mine. "The government."

My world tilted. The darkness I thought we'd vanquished was merely hiding, waiting to strike.

Did you love *The Family Of Deception*? Then you should read *The Genius Deaf: A true Story Of Triumph And Inspiration*[1] by Mirembe Allan!

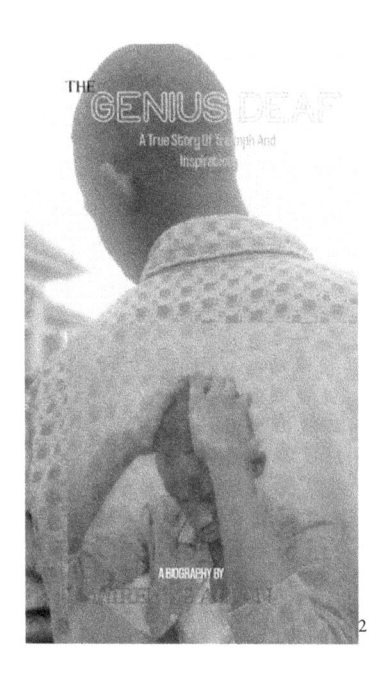

"In a world that often silenced him, Mirembe Allan found his voice. Born deaf, he faced a lifetime of isolation, frustration, and doubt. But he refused to let his disability define him.

With tears, sweat, and unwavering determination, Mirembe Allan shattered the barriers that stood between him and his dreams. He discovered a world of vibrant colors, of music that echoed in his soul, and of a love that knew no bounds.

---

1. https://books2read.com/u/49AG9Y

2. https://books2read.com/u/49AG9Y

This is a story of the human spirit's unbreakable will, of the power of hope and resilience, and of the triumph of the human heart. Mirembe Allan's journey will take you to the depths of sorrow and the heights of joy, leaving you breathless and yearning for more.

Through his eyes, you'll experience the agony of feeling invisible, the ecstasy of finding true connection, and the liberation of embracing one's true self. You'll laugh, you'll cry, and you'll cheer as Mirembe Allan overcomes the impossible and achieves the extraordinary.

"The Genius Deaf" is a testament to the transformative power of the human spirit, a reminder that our differences are our greatest strengths, and a call to arms to embrace our unique beauty. Get ready to be moved, inspired, and forever changed by this unforgettable true story."

About the Author

Allan D. Genius also known as Mirembe Allan is a USA Bestselling Author. He is also the founder of Allan IInternational Co. an organization for inspiring young minds and also a book publishing company. Despite the obstacles he faced because of his deafness due to a serious disease that he got in 2014, he never gave up on chasing his dreams and kept fighting even though life was hard for him living in a silent world.

About the Publisher

Allan Inspirations is an inspirational organization and an online book publishing company which was founded in 2021 by Mirembe Allan who also acts as it's president and CEO.

Milton Keynes UK
Ingram Content Group UK Ltd.
UKHW030900151124
451262UK00001B/22